Eva Ibbotson

Let Sleeping Sea-Monsters Lie... and Other Cautionary Tales

Illustrated by Sarah Horne

MACMILLAN CHILDREN'S BOOKS

First published 1983 by Macmillan Children's Books

This edition published 2012 by Macmillan Children's Books
a division of Macmillan Publishers Limited
20 New Wharf Road, London N1 9RR
Basingstoke and Oxford
Associated companies throughout the world
www.panmacmillan.com

ISBN 978-1-4472-0587-6

1 3 5 7 9 8 6 4 2

A CIP catalogue record for this book is available from
the British Library.

Printed and bound by CPI Group (UK) Ltd, Croydon CR0 4YY

To Ellen

Contents

Foreword

As long as stories and people have existed,
parents have been telling cautionary tales
to their children, warning them what
might happen to them if they are nasty,
reckless or just bad-mannered. But these
are cautionary tales with a difference. True,
the offenders have the usual vices – they are
rude, snobbish, disobedient,
aggressive and bossy – and
are bound to come a cropper. But
the way in which they get their
comeuppance is ingenious
in every case, and always
has something to do with

an imaginary monster. In these adventures you will be introduced to a Frid, a Kraken, a Boobrie and several other creatures populating Eva Ibbotson's fertile mind.

Eva Ibbotson, in common with some of my other favourite writers such as E. Nesbit and Roald Dahl, writes with a delightful mixture of wild imagination and down-to-earth common sense, tempering her flights of fancy with a satisfying sense of justice. These are the sort of stories I enjoyed as a child, which my children enjoyed and which I'm sure my grandchildren will enjoy too.

Julia Donaldson

The Worm and the Toffee-Nosed Princess

Once upon a time there lived a worm. Not an earthworm – earthworms are smooth and pink and soft with purple bulges in the middle. Not a tapeworm – tapeworms are white and flat and slippery and like to live inside people's stomachs if they can. Not a lugworm either – lugworms, which people use for fishing, stay buried in the sand.

No, this was a very different sort of worm. It was a great, long, hairy worm, and when I say "long" I mean as long as a

train or as two football pitches or as four thousand, three hundred and fifty pork sausages laid end to end. This worm had a forked tongue like so many monsters and a poisonous breath but it didn't have wings; it just slithered. Dragons have wings; worms don't. What it did have was the power to join itself up again when it was cut into pieces. It also had blue eyes which is unusual in a worm.

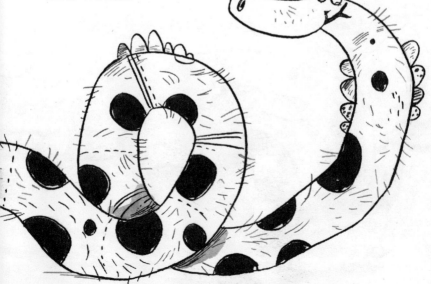

One day this worm was lying peacefully in a field. Its head was by the gate and its body was looped round and round and round the field it was in, and a bit over into the next field. And as the worm lay there, just thinking its own thoughts, the gate opened and a Princess walked in.

The Princess looked at the worm and the worm looked at the Princess. Then the

worm lifted its head, with its cornflower-blue eyes, and said:

"Good morning."

It did not say "Good morning" because it thought it was an enchanted prince and wanted the Princess to kiss it and turn it back into a prince. It knew perfectly well that it was not an enchanted prince. It said "Good morning" because it was a polite worm and that is what you say to people – and certainly to princesses – when they come through your front gate.

But the Princess did not say "Good morning" back. She made a rather rude gesture and then she said:

5

"Phooey!"

Now "Phooey" is not a nice thing to say to a worm when it has just said "Good morning" to you. The worm was amazed. It thought it had misheard. So it lifted its head to speak again.

"I said 'Good morning, Princess'," said the worm.

"And I," said the Princess, making an even ruder gesture, "said 'Phooey!'."

Now this worm was not particularly ferocious or troublesome but it *was* a worm.

Worms are like dragons or serpents: they are monsters and able to be fierce. So when the Princess said "Phooey" to it a second time, the worm did the only thing it could do. It shot out its forked and poisonous tongue, wrapped it round the Princess, pulled her into its mouth – and swallowed her. Then it went back to lying peacefully in the field.

Well, you can imagine the fuss in the palace when it was discovered that the Princess had disappeared.

"Where is the Princess?" shouted the King, and: "Where is my little girl?" wailed the Queen, and: "Where is Her Royal Highness?" yelled the servants.

Actually, the servants weren't at all sorry that

the Princess had gone because she'd been a very naughty child. She'd begun as one of those babies that turn purple from screaming and kick people in the stomach, and gone on to be the sort of little girl who yells with temper if she's asked to put on a pair of plain knickers instead of lace ones. Later she was faddy about her food and snobby with the children who came to play with her and rude to the servants. "Princess Toffee-Nose" they called her because that's just what she was.

But when it was discovered that the Princess had not only vanished, but been eaten by a worm, something had to be done. So the King sent out a proclamation

PROCLAMATION OF THE KING

HALF THE KINGDOM TREASURE FOR THE DEMISE OF GIGANTIC WORM

the King

to say that anyone could have half the treasure in his kingdom if he would go out and slay the loathsome monster who had devoured his daughter. He would also have offered his daughter's hand in marriage but of course he couldn't because she had been eaten by a worm.

Then he waited for lots of princes to come flocking to the palace, but nobody came at all. This was because the Princess had been rude to so many people that no one cared what happened to her and nobody wanted to risk being killed.

But at last they found a tired old Knight who said, "All right, I'll see what I can do."

So the Knight rode off on his rather battered old horse in his rather rusty armour to the field where the worm was still lying peacefully with his head by the gate and his body coiled round and round the field.

And because the Knight was a very fearless
knight he began at once to chop pieces off
the worm, starting at the tail. He chopped
off one piece and then another and another.
And every time he chopped off a piece he
threw it as far away as he could, over a hedge
or into a duck pond, because he thought that
if he did this the worm would not be able to
join itself up again. He didn't know, you see,

that he was dealing with a very clever worm.

At first the worm did not notice what was happening. This was because worms like that are so long that it takes ages for messages to get from one end to the other.

But in the end it did notice and then
a long and bloody fight began. The worm
reared round and snapped at the Knight
with its teeth and blew at him with its
poisonous breath and roared horribly. But
the Knight, though old, was nimble and the
Knight's armour,
though rusty,
was poison-
proof and he
just went on

leaping out of the worm's way and chopping
more and more bits off the worm and
throwing them away so that the poor worm
got weaker and weaker and weaker.

The Knight had got almost to the head end of the worm when something odd happened. He had just chopped off a rather fat and bulgy bit and was picking it up to throw it over the gate when there was a slithering, slurching kind of noise and out on to the grass fell the Princess!

She was in an awful mess! You know what the insides of squashed animals are like. Little bits of mince stuck to her all over. She was wet; she was crumpled; and she was bald, too, because the Knight had chopped so

close to her head that he had
cut off her hair. What's more,
she was covered in bright red
spots because inside the worm
she had got the measles.

Still, she was alive. So the Knight shook
her out and dried her and when he had
finished chopping up the worm he put her
over his saddle and rode back to the palace.

The King was terribly pleased. "You brave and noble Knight," he said. "I offer you my daughter's hand in marriage."

"No, thank you,"

said the Knight. "Your daughter is not at all the kind of person I should like to marry and anyway I am too old."

"She looks better when she's cleaned up," said the Queen.

"And when she hasn't got the measles," said the servants.

But the Knight went on shaking his
head. He didn't want half the King's treasure
either because it was too heavy and would
tire his horse. He just took three gold pieces
and rode away.

But what of the
poor worm? There it
lay in the middle of the field with
its sore, sad head chopped off in a
pool of blood and its cornflower-blue eyes
full of tears, and everywhere – strewn over
the hedges and the haystacks and the
bushes – its hacked-up pieces of body.

Slowly, bravely, all that day and the next
day and the next the worm went about
joining itself up and joining itself up and
joining itself up. It would get three bits
that fitted together and then the fourth bit
would roll away into the ditch and get lost
and it would have to hunt everywhere to
find it. Once, it had thirteen bits of its tail
all together but the fourteenth just couldn't

be found because the Knight had
thrown it into a tree and some rooks had
used it to hold meetings on. And the bit
the Princess had been in was particularly
difficult to fit on because it had got stretched
and flabby at the edges. But the worm just
worked and worked and worked . . .

Just before noon on the third day it
finished joining itself up and then it slithered
away over the fields and hills and valleys
till it came to a clear, deep lake because it

wanted to see what it looked like. But when it stared into the water and saw its reflection, the worm gasped with surprise.

It had made a sort of mistake. It had put its head in the *middle* and stretching away to either side of it, as long as *half* a train or *one* football pitch or two thousand, one hundred and seventy-five pork sausages, were its two bits of body. It had a body to the right of it and a body to the left of it and in the middle was its head.

For a while the worm just stared into the water and then a pleased and happy smile spread over its face and its cornflower-blue eyes danced with joy. And it said to itself: "It was a bad day when the Princess came and

said 'Phooey' to me and I swallowed her and
the Knight chopped me up but now I am
probably the only worm in the whole world
with a head in the middle of my long, long
body – and thus I shall remain until the end
of time!"

And thus it did.

As for the Princess, no one ever came to

marry her – not a prince or a plumber or
a roadmender or a window cleaner – not
anyone, because if you start life by kicking
people in the stomach and go on by yelling
with temper if you are supposed to wear
plain knickers instead of lace
ones and then say "Phooey" to
a worm, you are going to have
a very lonely life. Which is what
she did, and serve her right.

Never Steal
Milk from
a Frid

Mostly when you climb a hill or scramble through the heather and come across a large rock it will be just what it seems: a large rock.

But sometimes – just sometimes – you might come across a rock that is *not* exactly what it seems. Such a rock will look strange and sinister and different.

A rock like that will be a *Frid rock* and inside it there will be a *Frid*.

What a Frid looks like is very hard to say because Frids never come out of their rocks, but what they do is nasty (as you shall see).

Once there was a Frid rock on a hill above a village in which there lived about two hundred people, some cows, some chickens, some pigs – and five dogs. All the people in this village were very careful not

to upset the Frid. They spoke politely and
quietly when they went near the rock and
they put out crumbs by it and bowls of milk
because crumbs and milk are

what Frids like. And the
dogs were even more
well behaved than the
people, because an old
story said that the last time
a Frid had been angered it was by a dog and
though no one could remember what had
happened to the dog they knew that it was
bad.

The five dogs in the village were friends.
There was an Old English sheepdog with
wise eyes, which peered out under his grey

and white fringe of
hair. There was a liver-
coloured spaniel who
loved everybody and
wanted everybody to
love her, and spent a
lot of time on her back

with her legs in the air so that people could
stroke or scratch her or even kick her if
they wished. There was a basset hound with
a body like a hairy drainpipe and ears that
were full of little spiders and beetles which
had climbed in as he trailed them along the
ground. There was a poodle who had once
belonged to a travelling circus. And there
was a mongrel called Fred.

Every one of these dogs was a sensible dog. They knew that a Frid lived in the rock above their village and though they often went for walks together they took care to keep well away from the rock and if they did have to pass it, they did so quietly with their tails down. As for lifting their legs against anything within half a mile of the Frid rock, they would rather have died. Nor did the mongrel, though he was as tough as they came, ever make any jokes about a *Fred* not being afraid of a *Frid* because he knew that anyone who was not scared of a Frid was, quite simply, a fool.

And so for many years the people and the dogs in

the village lived in peace with the Frid and the Frid lived in peace with them, taking his crumbs and his milk at night and bothering no one.

Then one day a completely new dog arrived in the village. She came in a carriage with a rich and important lady who was staying in the inn and her name was Winsome Wilhelmina III of Bossybank Snootersloop, from which you will see that she was a

pedigree dog and very, very grand. Winsome had long blonde hair, masses and masses of it. She had hair on her back which flowed down to the ground on either side. She had hair on her legs and hair rippling along her tail and hair on her head, where it was gathered into a topknot and tied with a pink satin ribbon. When Winsome Wilhelmina walked (which she didn't very often because she preferred to be carried) she looked like a blonde wig on castors and all you could see apart from her hair were her snappy black eyes and her snooty black nose and, of course, her ribbon.

The other dogs saw her come and saw her carried into the inn, but they did not expect to see her again. She was obviously not the kind of dog who would mix with ordinary dogs like themselves. But it is no good being terribly grand and pure-bred and important if there is no one to see how grand and pure-bred and important you are and on the third day of her visit, Winsome Wilhelmina trotted out of the back door of the inn, found the five dogs lying in a patch of shade under a tree — and began at once to boast.

"I," said the new dog, "am Winsome Wilhelmina. My pedigree goes back for nine hundred years. I sleep in a basket lined with white satin and it takes my mistress's maid an hour to comb my hair."

"Goodness!" said the sheepdog.

"I only eat the best steak cut into finger-thin slices, and peeled grapes for my bowels," Winsome went on.

The other dogs had never seen grapes, let alone peeled grapes, but they were very

impressed and the spaniel grovelled in the dust and licked

Winsome Wilhelmina's toes.

"There are real diamonds in my collar," the little show-off continued. "You may look."

So the dogs peered at Winsome's neck and sure enough, buried deep in her silky, golden hair, was the sparkle of jewels.

By now the village dogs were quite overcome by the grandness of this newcomer. But Fred, the mongrel, plucked up his courage and said:

"Like to go for a walk with us, Win?"

Winsome Wilhelmina tossed her head.

"I'd prefer you to use my full name if you don't mind. But I don't mind going for a walk as long as there's no mud or dust to get in my hair."

So they took Winsome Wilhelmina for a walk.

Because they did not want her to get her beautiful coat muddy they did not take her for their usual walk along the river where there were water rats to be chased, and because they did not want her to get dried leaves in her long silky hair they did not take her into the woods where there were pigeons to be terrified and holes to dig. Instead, they took her up the clean, straight, sandy path that led towards the Rock of the Frid.

As they got closer to the rock, the village dogs got quieter and quieter but Winsome Wilhelmina didn't.

"What on earth is that absolutely extraordinary rock?" she said in her high, upper-class-dog voice.

"It's the Frid rock," said the sheepdog.

"It's best to be quiet when we go past it,"
said the basset hound.

"Quiet?" yapped Winsome piercingly.
"Why should I be quiet because of some
perfectly ridiculous rock? I've never even
heard of a Frid. I don't believe there is such
a thing!"

"There is, Winsome," said the sheepdog
seriously. "There really is such a thing as a
Frid and it's inside that rock."

"How do you know?" said Winsome, tossing her topknot.

"We know," said the poodle, "because of what it does. Especially to dogs."

"Pooh!" said Winsome. "Country dogs are always full of silly fancies."

She trotted on her stiff little legs right up to the base of the rock and began to snuffle at the crumbs the villagers had left. Then out shot her little pink tongue and one by one she gobbled them up!

The spaniel whimpered with terror.

"Come away," barked the mongrel.
"For heaven's sake, Winsome, come away
before it is too late!"

Winsome Wilhelmina took not the
slightest notice. Snuffling her way further
along the rock she found a saucer of fresh
milk.

"No!" yelped the basset hound. "Not the
Frid's milk! No, no, no!"

Winsome didn't even
bother to turn round.
Out came her greedy
little tongue again
and lap, lap, lap
she went until

every single drop of milk was gone.

And then – you will find this almost impossible to believe – she went and made a puddle beside the Rock of the Frid itself!

With a howl of terror, the other dogs fled. A frightful silence fell. The sky darkened; the earth trembled. And on the face of the Frid rock there appeared something so awful that no one

could give it a name. An eye – yet like no eye that has ever been seen. With a crack the rock split to form a mouth, a bottomless hole, a *something* that gaped and beckoned.

"*SCROOMPH!*" said the Frid. "*SQWILLOP!*"

And as it spoke these dreadful words, Winsome was lifted up bodily and sucked, slowly, into the hole.

The hole closed. The eye vanished, and Winsome Wilhemina had gone.

It was a long while before the whimpering dogs dared to crawl back again. But bravely they came and patiently they waited. They waited and they waited and

then the awful eye appeared once again and
the hole gaped open.

"GERTCH!" said the Frid. "PFOO!
BWERK!"

And out on to the ground it spat – a
thing.

Only what could it be? It was the size of a very small rat. It was quite raw and pink and totally naked. And as it lay there, like something on a butcher's slab, it seemed more dead than alive.

The Frid had closed up again. Slowly the dogs crawled forward and the spaniel began to lick the pitiful thing with her loving tongue.

"Good heavens!" said the sheepdog, when he could trust himself to speak again. "Look – it's her! It's Winsome! She's still wearing her collar."

It was true. On the
scalped, raw little rat of
an animal, the collar
of diamonds still
twinkled.

And in that
moment, the wise old sheepdog recalled
what his great-grandmother had told him
years and years before.

"I remember now," he said, "what a Frid
is. A Frid is *a thing that turns dogs hairless.*"

And the other dogs nodded, for it was
coming back to them, too, that if there is a
something that turns dogs hairless then that
something is a Frid.

So they dragged the poor, silly, hairless

little creature down to the village, and since her rich mistress wanted nothing to do with her now she was so ugly, the dogs themselves licked and loved her back to health. Winsome Wilhelmina became quite a nice dog but her hair never grew again, not so much as a single eyelash or a whisker. Nor could she ever speak about what had happened when she was inside the Frid. "Let sleeping Frids lie, my dears," was all she would say when visiting dogs came and asked her questions. That's all we dogs can do: just let them lie."

And I am happy to say they did.

Let Sleeping Sea-Monsters Lie

Of all the monsters in the world there is
none so fierce or so terrible as the Kraken.
A Kraken is the size of an island; it can eat
large ships at a single gulp and when it lashes
its tail, whole cities on the shore will be
flooded. If you just say the name "Kraken"
to the bravest sailor with the biggest muscles
and the largest anchor tattooed on his chest
he will probably faint from fright.

The Kraken I am going to tell you

about was, for many
years, as terrible
as any. He would

eat a galleon for breakfast, a man-of-war
for lunch, a pirate ship for supper, and still
sometimes gulp down a rowing boat for tea.
But one day he didn't want to go on like
this any more. The oars and
the sails that
he swallowed
were beginning to
scratch the inside
of his stomach
and the screams
of the sailors
as he sucked
them into his
mouth gave
him earache

and made him feel depressed. So he gorged himself on seaweed three times a day instead, which kept him perfectly healthy.

At the same time he decided to settle down because it is difficult to make friends if you are always roaring about and flooding things and swallowing them.

The place he chose to settle down was a peaceful, sunny bay with clear, deep water. The Kraken kept his neck and his huge, whiskery head with its big eyes, long eyelashes and intelligent forehead well down in the water and he kept his tail, which was scaly and interesting, in the water also, but he left his round, smooth back sticking out above the surface of the waves.

Soon he began to make friends. His head made friends with a mermaid who lived in a grotto not far from his chin. She was no

longer young and the songs she sang were rude because she had learned them from some sailors in a pub. This had happened when she came out on land for a while and married an innkeeper who had forced her to work as a barmaid. But standing on her tail all day made her tired and when her husband said she smelled fishy she had left him and returned to the water. She was a motherly mermaid and very fond of the Kraken and he of her. The Kraken also liked a rather dotty sea-witch who roared about

muttering spells which began with words like "Sweery, sweery linkum-loo" and usually ended with someone being turned into a sea cucumber. And he liked the sea horses and the peacefully squelching squids.

The Kraken's tail, which was about half a mile away from its head, didn't exactly make friends but the sea creatures made friends with it. Giant eels curled themselves round it and all those magic people that you find under the water – people whose front ends are horses and back ends are people, or whose back ends are fish and front ends are seals – used it to swing on and have fun.

With so many friends to talk to and enough seaweed to eat, the Kraken was

very happy. But because its head was so
busy at one end and its tail was so useful at
the other, the Kraken forgot about its back,

which was sticking hugely and humpily out of the water. And of course you will guess what happened next.

After about fifty years, grass seeds began to sprout on the Kraken's back and a meadow grew up, and among the grass the prettiest flowers – sea pinks and king-cups and forget-me-nots. Then a little larch tree managed to grow and another and another . . . and in the trees birds began

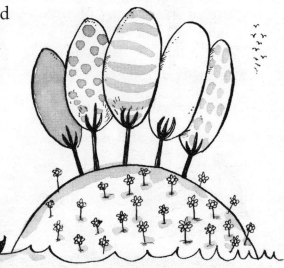

to nest and to sing and to lay little speckled eggs.

In short, the Kraken became the most beautiful and peaceful island you can imagine!

Naturally it was not long before people started rowing out from the village on the shore of the bay for picnics.

The Kraken did not mind this. The people who came were sensible and well behaved and would not have dreamed of leaving paper or broken glass about, and all that the Kraken

could feel as they walked about on him was a very gentle tickle which was not at all disagreeable.

Then one day a large boat rowed out to the island and in it were five ordinary, nice little girls in clean pinafores

with excited, shining eyes and five ordinary, sensible little boys in clean sailor suits with scrubbed and happy faces. These were the children of the village school on their Sunday Outing. Also in the boat were the children's teacher, who was called Miss Pigg but was not at all like a pig but very kind, Miss Pigg's mother, who was ninety-three, and two strong fishermen to do the rowing.

And if these had been the only people in the boat everything would have been all right, but they were not. There was also a truly awful boy called Algernon.

It is quite possible that there has never been a child as unpleasant as this boy. Algernon lied and cheated. He kicked and bullied. When Miss Pigg tried

to teach him to read he yawned or dribbled or fell off his stool and when he saw a stray kitten or a puppy in the school yard he pelted it with stones. But Algernon, too, was at the village school so he could not be left out of The Outing.

The boat landed. Miss Pigg's old mother was placed on a tussock with her parasol open against the sun. Miss Pigg began to butter the sandwiches. And the five sensible little boys and the five well-behaved little girls ran about, so happy they thought they would burst. They took off their shoes and they paddled. They made daisy chains. They crawled through the grass pretending to be Ferocious Animals.

But not Algernon. Algernon was bored.
He kicked the stones about and hit one of
the little boys on the forehead. He pulled
down a thrush's nest and
trampled on the eggs. He
found a little girl with
her apron full of cowrie
shells and threw them on
the ground.

"I'm bored," he moaned. "There's nothing to do on this island."

But after lunch, when everyone was resting, he did find something to do. He thought of it because it was the one thing Miss Pigg had told the children not to do on the island.

"You must not light a fire, children," she had said, "because it is dangerous and will damage the plants and trees."

And the five little girls and the five little boys had listened and nodded their heads. But not Algernon.

He gathered some sticks and he piled up some dry grass right in the middle and humpiest bit of the island. Then he crept to where one of the fishermen was sleeping and stole his matches. And then . . . he lit a fire!

The fire started small. But soon it caught a gust of wind and it grew and it spread.

At first the Kraken felt nothing at all. Then it felt rather a strong tickle . . . then an itch . . . and then a pain!

"Ow!" said the Kraken, feeling very much upset.

Well, you will see what happened next and it is no use at all blaming the Kraken. If someone lit a fire on you, what would you do?

The Kraken sank.

He sank very slowly, because he was a monster who did not do things in a hurry, but he sank. And on the island the children saw the water rise over
the fringe of sand, on to
the grass, and up and
up into the button
boots of Miss Pigg's
mother sitting
underneath
her
parasol . . .

"To the boats, children! Quick! Quick!"
cried Miss Pigg.

She gathered up the smallest of the little
girls and the smallest of the little boys and,
with the rest of the children following
her, she ran to where the fishermen
were waiting in the boat. Miss
Pigg's mother, who was too old to
run, climbed into her upturned
parasol and floated towards
the boat where the fishermen
hauled her to safety.

But
Algernon
was still in
the middle
of the island,
shouting and
hooting round
his fire.

"Algernon!"
shouted Miss
Pigg, standing up in the boat and waving her
arms. "Algernon, come quickly!"

Too late! The island – and the boy – had
gone!

Down and down went awful Algernon,
down into the icy water . . . down and down

he sank until he was level with the Kraken's gaping mouth.

The Kraken had of course meant to swallow Algernon, but when he saw the soggy, pulpy boy he said: "I find I do not want to eat this child."

"Can't say I blame you," said the mermaid. "I wouldn't fancy him myself. But what's to be done with him? They don't last more than a few minutes under water and we don't want dead bodies littering up the place."

"Perhaps the sea-witch could turn him into something?" suggested the Kraken.

"Good idea," said the mermaid. "I'll get her." And she swam off very quickly because Algernon was fast becoming waterlogged and magic does not work on people who are dead.

So the sea-witch came and did her spell, the one that began "Sweery, sweery linkum-loo", and she turned Algernon into the thing he most reminded her of, which was a sea slug with a slimy body and blotchy spots.

As for the children and Miss Pigg and

 Miss Pigg's mother and the

fishermen in the village,

they were at first upset

at losing their beautiful

island. But when they

realised that it had been

a Kraken they became

very excited. Soon

people came from all over

the world and gave the fishermen a lot of

money to row them out to where the island

had been. So the fishermen became rich and

bought lovely clothes for their wives and

nice toys for their children and were very

happy. The Kraken, too, was happy because

he had no more trouble with his back.

But whether Algernon was happy or not I cannot tell you. Some things are easy and some things are difficult – and finding out whether a sea slug is happy is very difficult indeed!

The Boobrie and
the Sheepish
Scotsmen

Once upon a time three Scotsmen were
walking through the Highlands on a cold
winter's day when they came across some most
unusual footprints in the snow. They were the
tracks of webbed feet with curved claws on the
end and each track was absolutely enormous,
about the size of a house.

"Now what on earth can that be?" said Chief MacGregor, a tall, thin Scotsman with scars on his hairy knees from fighting in a battle.

"Whatever it is, it's mighty large," said Chief MacCallum, a small, fat Scotsman whose stomach bulged roundly beneath his kilt.

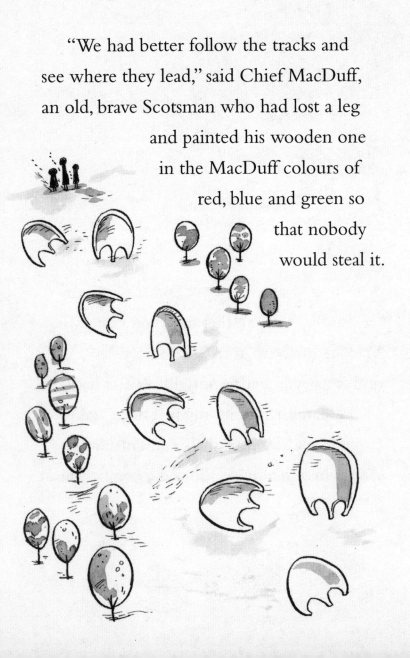

"We had better follow the tracks and
see where they lead," said Chief MacDuff,
an old, brave Scotsman who had lost a leg
and painted his wooden one
in the MacDuff colours of
red, blue and green so
that nobody
would steal it.

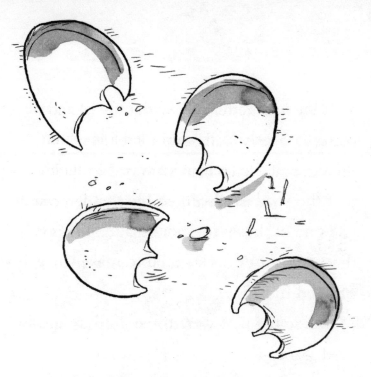

So they followed the tracks of the
webbed feet which looked as though
whatever had made them was not only
gigantic but also a bit knock-kneed and
pigeon-toed because they pointed inwards.
And when they had followed them for about

an hour they came to a lake (only of course, being in Scotland, it was called a loch). At the edge of the loch there was the biggest nest they had ever seen, so big that it looked like one of those stockades made of logs that the settlers in America used to make to keep off Red Indians.

Inside the nest were three fluffy, round-eyed, goofy-looking chicks with mottled feathers and yellow beaks. However, when I say "chicks" I do not mean anything sweet and little and quaint. These chicks were the size of full-grown elephants, and as they jostled against each other and opened their huge beaks, the noise that came out was not "CHEEP!" but "BAA!"

The Scotsmen looked at each other
and their knees beneath their kilts began to
tremble because they knew they had been
following the tracks of a BOOBRIE bird
and that these chicks were Boobrie chicks.
They also knew that the chicks were saying
"Baa!" instead of "Cheep!" because what
Boobries feed on, mostly, is sheep.

"What are we going to do?" quavered
tall, thin MacGregor.

"The Boobrie will carry away all our livestock!" squeaked small, fat MacCallum.

"We must make a plan," said brave MacDuff, striking his wooden leg with his walking stick.

So the Scotsmen walked back to their village and thought out what to do. They were quite right to be afraid. The Boobrie, which is a very Scottish bird, may not be very clever but it is so big that it seems to fill the whole sky when it appears and it is so strong that it can swoop down and carry off a sheep or a horse or a cow as easily as you could pick a daisy. A Boobrie's eyes are round and black and crazy-looking, its beak is the size of a canoe, and when it flies it makes a mournful, honking noise like a foghorn with stomach ache.

So the three Scotsmen thought and thought about what to do and then brave old MacDuff struck his forehead and said:

"I know! We will disguise ourselves as sheep and when the Boobrie swoops down on us we will shoot it with our horse pistols."

"And our blunderbusses!" yelled thin MacGregor.

"In its soft underbelly!" cried brave MacDuff.

Fat MacCullum didn't say anything because the idea of pretending to be a sheep and popping off bullets at the Boobrie made *his* poor underbelly quiver like a jelly. But he did not wish to seem a coward so all three

Scotsmen began then and there to dress up as sheep.

This was difficult. First they had to find some sheepskins that fitted over their backs and then they had to go down on their

hands and knees and see if they looked like sheep which mostly they didn't. MacDuff didn't because you don't often get sheep with wooden legs, and MacCallum didn't because he was so fat that he bulged out pinkly underneath like a sausage does when you fry it without pricking it first. And MacGregor *certainly* didn't because he had forgotten to take off his sporran and sheep with sporrans are very, very rare.

But in the end, by pulling and pushing at the skins and sticking extra bits of wool here and there they didn't look quite so bad and when they had practised saying "Baa" a few times they set off for the moor above the loch where they had first seen the Boobrie

tracks. They didn't like to walk upright
carrying their sheepskins in case the Boobrie
was watching, so they crawled, and they had
a very nasty time. Crawling in the snow
is nasty anyway, and crawling in the snow
while pretending to be a sheep and carrying
a horse pistol, a blunderbuss and a catapult is
even nastier. The Scotsmen fell and stumbled
and their poor hairy legs, which weren't
quite covered by the sheep hides, turned

blue with cold. When they tried to say "Baa" their teeth rattled like doors in a high wind. But they crawled on till they reached the moor and then they huddled together and waited.

They did not wait for long.

The Boobrie did not come from the sky. It rose from the waters of the lake and the sight was one to turn the bravest man to stone. First came its head with its mad, round, staring eyes and then its terrible beak, curved like a pelican's to carry its prey, then its gigantic feathered body rising like a living island from the water and lastly its webbed and house-sized feet.

It was the mother Boobrie. She was

hungry and she was worried about
her chicks and as she circled the moor,
darkening the sky with her huge wings and
making the mournful, honking noise that
Boobries make, her crazy eyes searched
anxiously for something to give them
to eat. Round and round flew the
Boobrie, searching and honking,
and presently the vast and
worried bird
saw exactly
what she was
looking for.
Three sheep.

The Boobrie did not
smile because birds don't
but she was very pleased.
One sheep would have
been good, two would
have been better but
three sheep – one for
each of her chicks –
was perfect. She
circle once and
dived down on
to the moor.

This was the moment the Scotsmen had
been waiting for. They had got it all planned.
As the bird came down they were going to
step out from under their sheepskins, point

their horse pistol and their blunderbuss and
their catapult at the soft underbelly of the
bird – and fire!

What actually happened was different.
As the Boobrie
swooped towards
MacDuff, the
brave Scotsman
tried to lift his
gun, got the catch
wedged against his
wooden leg and
let loose a rain
of bullets into a
frozen cow pat.
Tall MacGregor

managed to get his
arm out and shoot off
the blunderbuss but
though he had filled
it from a tin labelled
Black Bullets these
were not proper
bullets but a dark
kind of peppermint
which has the same
name – and if there
is one thing you
cannot kill a
Boobrie with it is
a rain of peppermints. As for fat MacCallum,
he had fainted clean away before he

could loose off his catapult with the brass bedknob which he had brought to fire at the Boobrie's heart.

The Boobrie, who was a bit short-sighted, did not notice any of these things. All she noticed were three ordinary, though rather wiggly, sheep.

So first she swooped on brave MacDuff and picked him up and flew with him to the nest by the loch and dropped him down in front of Chick Number One. Then she flew back and swooped down on the skinny MacGregor sheep and dropped him down in front of Chick Number Two. And lastly she went back for the MacCallum sheep which was a very quiet sheep because the fat Scotsman was still in a faint.

After this the Boobrie felt very pleased with herself and waited for the chicks to

start eating
the sheep
she had
so kindly
brought
them.

But they
didn't. The chicks
looked down with
their goofy pop-eyes
at the sheep. They bent their
scraggy necks. They pecked at the
sheep with their yellow beaks and turned
them over with their webbed feet. And then
they looked reproachfully at their mother.

"Not nice," said Chick Number One.

"Smells nasty," said
Chick Number Two.

And Chick Number
Three, who was
the youngest, just said
gloomily: "Legs."

"Hairy," explained the
first chick to its mother.
"Hairy legs."

"And wooden,"
said Chick
Number
Two, picking at the
MacDuff sheep.

"Pink faces," said
the youngest chick, who

was taking it hard. It turned over the top end of the MacCallum sheep with its beak. "Horrid," it said, choking a little.

An anxious look spread over the mother Boobrie's face. She peered down at the nest, turned over MacDuff and lifted the sheepskin off MacCallum who had come out of his faint and was making a lot of noises, none of which were "Baa!"

The chicks were right. These were not proper sheep. A mistake had been made. And when you have made a mistake there is only one thing to do: put it right.

So the mother Boobrie picked up MacDuff in his sheepskin, carried him high in her beak and dropped him with a splash into the loch.

Next she picked up the MacGregor sheep, carried him high and dropped him into the loch.

Then she went back for the MacCallum
sheep and dropped him into the loch too.

And then she went flapping away on her
enormous wings to go and look for some
proper sheep because a mother's work is
never done.

As for the Scotsmen, they managed to
swim ashore and to hobble home, one in
his underpants, one in his vest to which a
frozen frog had stuck, and one in nothing
but a large leaf, and for the rest of the year
they had chilblains in places it would not be
polite to mention. MacDuff's wooden leg
was lost in the water and so were all the rest
of their things, which serves them right for
trying to trick a Boobrie bird. Boobries may

be a little silly, but if you give them
time they can always tell a Scotsman from
a sheep.

The Brollachan
Who Kept Mum

This is a story about a Brollachan.

You will now want to know what a Brollachan is and I will tell you. A Brollachan is a dark, splodgy, shapeless thing. It has two red eyes, an enormous mouth and absolutely nothing else whatsoever. A Brollachan has no bones and no stomach and no nose. It has no arms and no legs and no feet and no toes and therefore no toe-nails. And it has no hair. There is probably nothing with less hair than a Brollachan.

A Brollachan, then, is just a squashy and quite frightening blob which rolls about the place. But though it has no shape of its own a Brollachan can take on the shape of things that it meets. A Brollachan lying on a table,

for example, might become table-shaped
or a Brollachan looking at a round Dutch
cheese could become cheese-shaped if it
wished. And though it cannot really think it
can hear a little through its bulges and it can
certainly feel.

The Brollachan that this story is about lived in a house beside a swampy pond with his mother, who was a Fuath. Fuaths are evil and bad-tempered fairies who live near water, so they are often dripping wet. They look almost like ordinary ladies but if you

look at them carefully you will find that there is something odd about them. Sometimes they are hollow from behind, and sometimes they have only one nostril.

The Brollachan's mother had a long nose with a black wart on it, whiskery ears, one frightful long tooth and webbed feet. She was a worrier and she was a nagger. She wanted the Brollachan to be more scary and more shapeless than he was. She wanted him to lure people into the swamp by terrifying them with his vile red eyes. She wanted him to bubble disgustingly in the mud at the bottom of the pond and she wanted him to speak.

"Say 'Mummy'," she would yell at him. "Go on, say it. Say 'Mummy'."

But the Brollachan couldn't say "Mummy". He couldn't say anything. His mouth was big but he used it for eating, not for talking. So he would roll away sadly

and suck in a large turnip or a dead rat or
a ham-bone and you would see them – the
turnip or the rat or the ham-bone – lying
inside him sort of glowing a little until they
gradually became part of the Brollachan
because that is what happens to the things
that Brollachans eat.

All day long the Brollachan's mother followed him about, flapping a wet cloth at the furniture and dripping water on him.

"I don't know what will become of you, Brollachan. Why aren't you outside drowning someone? Why are you sitting in that bucket? Why don't you do something with your life? And why don't you say 'Mummy'?"

The Brollachan tried hard to please her. But however wide he opened his mouth, all that came out was a kind of gulp or a sort of glucking noise.

Sometimes the Brollachan's mother invited her friends round; ladies like Black Annis who was a cannibal witch with a blue

face or the Hag of the Dribble who was covered all over in grey slime, and then she would start.

"You don't know how I worry about him," she would say to these ladies, prodding the Brollachan with her webbed foot as he lay politely on the floor. "I can't sleep for worrying about him. He's so backward; he doesn't even try to frighten people into fits.

And he won't say 'Mummy'!"

"You should punish him," said the cannibal witch, burping rudely because she always swallowed people whole and this gave her wind. "Make him kneel on dried peas – nothing more painful than that!"

Which was not only a cruel but a silly thing to say since the Brollachan did not have any knees.

One day the Brollachan and his mother went for a walk in the forest. The Brollachan liked the forest very much. It was not wet like the swamp where he lived and the leaves felt pleasantly tickly under his body. He stretched himself out more and more and became bush-shaped, then tree-shaped, and

then just Brollachan-shaped but extra large. He felt happy and he felt free.

But the Brollachan's mother was still talking. "Why don't you learn the names of the trees, Brollachan?" she said. "Why don't you at least try to give off an evil mist? There's a Brollachan in the next valley who has a whole village gibbering with fright

every time he shows himself. *And* he can say
'Mummy'!"

After a while the Brollachan rolled away
between the trees and he rolled and he
rolled and he rolled until he was quite a way
from his mother.

The Brollachan's mother did not notice
this at first because she was so busy talking.

"It's all right for you," she said. "You can't have a stomach ache from worrying because you haven't got a stomach. You can't have a headache from worrying because you haven't got a head. You can't – Brollachan, where are you? Brollachan, come here at once, I'm talking to you. How dare you hide from your mother! I can see your vile red eyes behind that tree. I know you're just pretending to be that smelly toadstool. Now come to your mummy, Brollachan; come at once!"

But the Brollachan was a long, long way away and he was well and truly lost. He rolled on, however, until he came to a little wooden house in a clearing and because he

was very tired by now, he oozed through the
crack under the door and went inside.

It was a very nice house. There was a
fire in the grate and a painted stool and a
rocking chair in one corner. In the rocking
chair, fast asleep, sat an old man with a kind
face and a long white beard. Everything
was quiet and everything was dry and

the Brollachan liked it very much. And becoming more or less the shape of the hearthrug he lay down by the fire, closed his vile red eyes and fell asleep.

He slept for one hour and he slept for two while outside in the forest his mother, the Fuath, roared about on her webbed feet, searching and scolding and calling him. Goodness knows how long he might have gone on sleeping but just then a burning coal fell out of the fireplace and landed on one of the Brollachan's bulges.

Now the Brollachan couldn't talk but he could scream – and scream he did!

Everything then happened at once. The old man woke, saw that there was a

Brollachan on his hearthrug and jumped from his rocking chair. The Brollachan's mother heard the scream and rushed in at

the front door, dripping and shouting as she
came.

"What's happened to you, Brollachan?

How did you get here? Who hurt you? Has
that nasty old man hurt you? Have you hurt

my Brollachan, you stupid
old man? Because if you
have I'll turn you into
a bat with
bunions.
I'll turn
you into an eel with

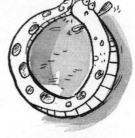

earache. I'll claw you into
strips of raw beef, I'll make

newts come out of
your nostrils,
I'll . . ."
On and
on she raged.

The old man did not know how to bear so much noise. He took his long white beard and stuffed the left half of it into his left ear and the right half of it into his right ear but still he could hear the Fuath's voice. Feeling quite desperate he got a broom and tried to shoo the Fuath out of doors.

But the Fuath would not be shushed and she would not be shooed. She just dripped and she threatened and she *talked*.

The Brollachan by now was very upset. His burn did not hurt any longer but he felt that things were not as they should be. His red eyes were wide with worry and his shapeless darkness shivered at all this unpleasantness. What he wanted more than anything was to make things all right.

So he made himself very big and he opened his mouth and he went right up to his mother, who was still talking and scolding and waving her arms. If only he could do it! If only he could do the thing she wanted so much! Wider he opened his mouth and wider . . . and closer he went to his mother and closer . . . and harder he tried and harder . . . harder than he had ever tried in his whole life.

And then at last he did it. He actually did it!

"MUMMY!" said the Brollachan. "MUM – gluck – gulp!"

Then he stopped. His mother was not there.

The Brollachan was puzzled. He looked under the stool and behind the door but there was no sign of her. But though he was puzzled, he was not worried. He felt very close to his mother. And because it made him tired to be so clever he lay down again – but further from the fire – and fell asleep.

The old man took half his beard out of his right ear and half his beard out of his left ear and came over to have a look. He could see the Brollachan's mother inside the Brollachan as clear as clear. He could even see the wart on the end of her nose. She

was still talking and talking and talking but
Brollachans are soundproof so he couldn't
hear a thing.

So he smiled and nodded at the Brollachan as if to say, yes, you can stay, and went back to his rocking chair. The next day he made a fireguard so that the Brollachan wouldn't get burnt. And then he and the Brollachan lived together very happily. Because both of them had said all they were ever going to say and each was happy to let the other be the kind of person that he was.

Eva Ibbotson

Monster Mission

'We must kidnap some children,' announced Aunt Etta. 'Young, strong ones. It will be dangerous, but it must be done.'

Three children are stolen and taken to a bizarre island, which is home to some extraordinary creatures – including mermaids, selkies and the legendary kraken. The island is the base for a very mysterious mission, but the adventurers find themselves in perilous danger when it is suddenly under siege. Can they save themselves and their new friends?

To read an exciting extract from *Monster Mission* just turn the page . . .

Chapter One

Kidnapping children is not a good idea. All the same, sometimes it has to be done.

Aunt Etta and Aunt Coral and Aunt Myrtle were not natural kidnappers. For one thing, they were getting old and kidnapping is hard work; for another, though they looked a little odd, they were very caring people. They cared for their ancient father and for their shrivelled cousin Sybil who lived in a cave and tried to foretell the future – and most particularly they cared for the animals on the island on which they lived, many of which were quite unusual.

Some of the creatures that made their way to the Island had come far across the ocean to be looked after, and lately the aunts had felt that they could not go on much longer without help. And 'help' didn't mean grown-ups who were set in their ways. Help meant children who were young and strong and willing to learn.

So on a cool blustery day in April the three aunts gathered round the kitchen table and decided to go ahead. Some children had to be found and they had to be brought to the island, and kidnapping seemed the only sensible way to do it.

'That way we can choose the ones that are suitable,' said Aunt Etta. She was the eldest; a tall, bony woman who did fifty press-ups before breakfast and had a small but not at all unpleasant moustache on her upper lip.

The others looked out of the window at the soft green turf, the sparkling sea, and sighed, thinking of what had to be done. The sleeping powders, the drugged hamburgers, the bags and sacks and cello cases they would need to carry the children away in . . .

'Will they scream and wriggle, do you suppose?' asked Aunt Myrtle, who was the youngest. She suffered from headaches and hated noise.

'No, of course not. They'll be unconscious,' said Aunt Etta. 'Flat out. I don't like it any more than you do,' she went on, 'but you saw the programme on TV last week.'

The others nodded. When they first came to the Island they hadn't had any electricity, but after his hundredth birthday their father's toes had started to turn blue because not enough blood got to his feet and they had ordered a generator so that he could have an electric blanket. After that they thought they might as well have an electric kettle, and then a TV.

But the TV had been a mistake because of the nature programmes. Nature programmes always end badly. First you see the hairy-nosed wombats frisking about with their babies and then five minutes before the end you hear that there are only twelve breeding pairs left in the whole of Australia. Or there are pictures of the harlequin frogs of Costa Rica croaking away on their lily leaves and the next minute you are told that they're doomed because their swamps are being drained. Worst of all are the

4

rainforests. The aunts could never see a programme about the rainforests without crying, and last week there had been a particularly bad one with wicked people burning and slashing the trees, and pictures of the monkeys and the jaguars rushing away in terror.

'What if *we* became extinct?' Aunt Coral had wondered, blowing her nose. 'Not just the wombats and the harlequin frogs and the jaguars, but *us*.'

The others had seen the point at once. If a whole rainforest can become extinct why not three elderly ladies? And if they became extinct what would happen to their work and who would care for the creatures that came to the Island in search of comfort and of care?

There was another thing which bothered the aunts. Lately the animals that came to the Island simply wouldn't go away again. Long after they were healed they stayed on – it was almost as if they knew something – and that made more and more work for the aunts. There was no doubt about it, help had to be brought in, and quickly.

So now they were deciding what to do.

'How do we find the *right* children?' asked Myrtle as she looked longingly out at the point where the seals were resting. One of the seals, Herbert, was her special friend and she would very much rather have been out there playing her cello to him and singing her songs.

'We shall become *Aunts*,' said Etta firmly, settling her spectacles on her long nose.

The others looked at her in amazement. 'But we *are* aunts,' they said. 'How can we *become* them?'

This was true. There had been five sisters who had come to the Island with their father many years ago. They had found a ruined house and deserted beaches with only the footprints of sandpipers and dunlins on the sand, and barnacle geese resting on the way from Greenland, and the seals, quite unafraid, coming out of the water to have their pups.

They had started to repair the house, and planted a garden, and then one day they had found an oiled seabird washed up on a rock . . . Only it turned out not to be an oiled seabird. It was oiled all right, but it was something quite different – and after that they realized that they had been called to the Island by a Higher Power and that they had found their life's work.

But one of the sisters, Betty, had not cared for the Island. She hated the wind and the rain and the fish scales in her tea and the eider ducklings nesting in her bedroom slippers and she had gone away and got married to a tax inspector in Newcastle upon Tyne and now she lived in a house with three kinds of toilet freshener in the loo, and sprays to make her armpits smell nice, and not a fish scale in sight.

But the point was that she had two children. They were horrible, but they were children. She called the boy Boo-Boo and the girl Little One (though they had proper names of course). But horrible though they were, they were children and because of this her sisters had become aunts since all you have to do to become an aunt is have nephews and nieces.

Which is why now the sisters looked so surprised and said: 'But we *are* aunts.'

'Not that kind,' said Etta impatiently. 'I mean the

kind that live in an office or an agency and call themselves things like *Useful Aunts* or *Universal Aunts* or *Aunts Inc.* – the kind that parents pay to take their children to school and to the dentist, or to sit with them when they are ill.'

'Why don't the parents do it themselves?' asked Myrtle.

'Because they're too busy. People used to have real aunts and grandmothers and cousins to do it all, but now families are too small and real aunts go to dances and have boyfriends,' said Etta, snorting.

Coral nodded her head. She was the arty one, a large plump person who fed the chickens in a feather boa and interesting jewellery, and at night by the light of the moon she danced the tango.

'It's a good idea,' she said. 'You would be able to pick and choose the children – you don't want to end up with a Boo-Boo or a Little One.'

'Yes, but if the parents are truly fond of the children we shouldn't do it,' said Myrtle, pushing back her long grey hair.

'Well of course not,' said Etta. 'We don't want a hue and cry.'

'But if the children are nice the parents *would* be fond of them,' said Myrtle. 'And if they aren't we don't want them either.'

Etta sniffed. 'You'd be surprised. There are children all over the place whose parents don't know how lucky they are.'

They went on talking for a long time but no one could think of anything better than Etta's plan – not if the position of the Island was to be kept secret, and there was nothing more important than that.

There was one more aunt who would have been useful – not the one with the three kinds of toilet freshener, who was no use for anything – but Aunt Dorothy, who was next in age to Etta and would have been just the sort of person to have on a kidnapping expedition. But Dorothy was in prison in Hong Kong. She had gone out there to stop a restaurant owner from serving pangolin steaks – pangolins are beautiful creatures and are getting rare and should never be eaten – and Dorothy had got annoyed and hit the restaurant owner on the head with his own wok, and they had put her in prison. She was due out in a month but in the meantime only the three of them could go on the mission and they weren't at all sure about Myrtle because she was not very good out in the world and when she was away she always pined for Herbert.

'Are you sure you wouldn't rather stay behind, Myrtle?' said Coral now. But Myrtle had decided to be brave and said she thought that she should come along and do her bit.

'Only we won't say anything to Daddy,' said Etta. 'After all, kidnapping is a crime and he might worry.'

Captain Harper lived upstairs in a big bed with a telescope, looking out to sea. They had mostly given up telling him things. For one thing, he was stone deaf so that explaining anything took a very long time, and for another, as soon as he saw anybody he started telling them stories about what life had been like when he was a boy. They were good stories but every single aunt had heard them about three hundred times so they didn't hang around if they could help it.

But they did go and tell the Sybil. She was the old cousin who had come to the Island soon after them. Sybil was bookish and one day she had read a book about Greek mythology and about a person called *the* Sybil (not just Sybil) who was a prophetess and could foretell the future. So she had started prophesying about the weather, mumbling on about depressions over Iceland and the wind-chill factor and really she didn't get it wrong much more often than the weathermen on the telly. Then she had gone on to other things, and had gone to live in a cave with bats because that was where prophetesses were supposed to live, and had stopped washing because she said washing would weaken her powers, so that she was another person one did not visit for too long.

When the aunts told her that they were going to the mainland to kidnap some children the Sybil got quite excited. Her face turned blue and her hair began to stand on end and for a moment they hoped that she was going to tell them something important about the journey.

But it turned out that what she was foreseeing was squally showers, and what she said was 'take seasick pills', which they had decided to do anyway for the boat.

They still had to make sure that their cook, who was called Art, knew exactly what to do while they were away on their mission. Art was an escaped convict who had been washed up in a rowing boat on their shore. He had killed a man when he was young, and now he wouldn't kill anything with arms or legs or eyes – not even a shrimp – but he made excellent porridge. Then they gathered together all the things they would need: chloroform and sleeping powders and anaesthetizing darts which they used for stunning animals that were injured so that they could set their limbs. All of them had things to carry the children away in: Aunt Etta had a canvas holdall and Aunt Coral had a tin trunk with holes bored into it and Aunt Myrtle had her cello case. As they waited for the wind to change so that they could sail the *Peggoty* to the next island and catch the steamer, they were terribly excited.

It was a long and difficult journey – many years ago the army had tried to use the Island for experiments in radio signals and so as to keep its position secret they had changed the maps and forbidden boats to come near it. In the end they hadn't used it after all but it was still a forgotten place and the aunts meant to see that it stayed that way.

'Of course it won't be a real kidnap because we shan't ask the parents for a ransom,' said Etta.

'It'll be more of a child snatch,' Coral agreed.

But whether it was a kidnap or a child snatch, it was still dangerous and wicked, and as they waved goodbye to the Island their hearts were beating very fast.

Read more spooky, fantastical adventures by Eva Ibbotson

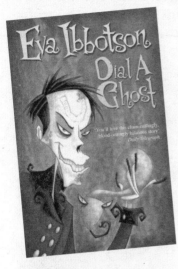

Read more spooky, fantastical
adventures by Eva Ibbotson